Lesbian Sex With The Dominant Bartender

Lesbian Age Gap Erotica

Kitty Keen

Contents

Lesbian Sex With The Dominant Bartender

My husband's a decent man, but he's also kinda useless. Not in a bad way, exactly. He earns well enough, he's good-looking, and fairly driven at his job. He even takes the garbage out most times. Sometimes, without me reminding him.

We married almost straight out of high school, and we don't have any kids yet, but here we are. I've just turned 22 but I swear Trevor's the only child I'll ever need. Or get.

They say guys don't reach full maturity until 25. So I hear, anyway. Which means I might still have a few years of this...whatever-ness.

Despite the fact I also have a full time job, I end up having to make all the decisions, pay all the bills, organize insurance. The list goes on and on, and I don't remember ever signing up for that shit. It's sapping my spirit in ways I didn't expect to happen for another 20 years.

These once-a-month girls' nights out are the one thing saving my sanity. I don't even bring my cellphone anymore, since Trevor inevitably calls me three times *minimum* to ask me where I hid something. Something that always ends up sitting right in fucking front of his lame face, if only he'd do more than take a cursory boy-look.

Trouble is, the group of girls is getting smaller and smaller, as more of them fall pregnant or just get too busy. 10 became 8, 8 became 5, and tonight there's only been 4 of us. It feels as if life's just passing me by while they all get to level up.

We're at our usual place. A small local bar, run by a guy who looks like the quintessential badass. Tall, broad, tatts out the wazoo. Frankly, he scares the crap out of me.

But even more scary is his barmaid. I don't know if she's the guy's sister, or wife, or mistress, or what. But even though she's tiny compared to him, she's cut from the same cloth.

She looks closer to 40 than 30, but that's more about the way she carries herself than the way she dresses. Her black, sleeveless T shows off the ink on her arms, and some more coming up onto her throat. Blonde hair dyed blue-green in places. She just exudes toughness. Control.

As I drink with the few other girls who actually turned up tonight, I can't stop following that barmaid with my eyes. Crossing and uncrossing my legs as she serves drinks. Gasping in awe as she not only puts up with all the dirty, insulting and sexist comments from her customers...but she actually fires straight back at them. And always with a half-grin on her striking face.

When a fight breaks out near us—this place has really gone to hell, lately—it's her, the barmaid, who steps in and breaks them up. And though I'm straight as a damn ruler, I fall a little bit in love with her.

One by one, my drinking companions peel away into the night. Back to their unsatisfying homes, with their sleepwalking husbands. Exactly what I have to look forward to.

And maybe that's why I can't stop staring at the chick behind the bar. Especially when she comes out from back there. That short black skirt hugs her curvy ass and lets me see the ink coming down the outsides of her thighs as well.

In short, even though she and I are about the same size, that woman is everything I'm not. I can't imagine a single situation where she's not completely large and in charge.

Before I realize it, I'm the last one standing. Well, sitting and swaying. And I'm, like, four drinks in. No way I can drive home, now.

The place is almost empty, and big badass dude is stacking chairs. Even I can take that hint.

I head over to the bar, to ask them if they'll call me a cab. And she's the only one back there. My woman-crush. My fascination.

It suddenly occurs to me that this will be the first time I've actually spoken to her.

"Hey, uh, hi. I'm Joannie."

She greets me with a lopsided smile that I can't quite read. It seems warm, and yet dismissive. As if that's even possible.

"Hiya, Joannie. I can't serve you anymore, sorry. We're just closing up." She reaches across and puts her hand over mine, and there's more of that fascinating ink, on her forearm, wrist, the back of her hand and even her fingers.

I catch myself staring, and then I recover. "Oh, uh...no. I just realized I've had a couple too many. Was wondering if you could call me a cab, please?"

Her smile grows broader, and only then do I notice the stud in her bottom lip. She slides her hand, brushing her fingertips down to mine, then coming back up.

"That's a real pretty ring," she says as she fingers it. "Your husband can't come get you?"

I try not to, but I scoff anyway. "Please. He'll be comatose in front of the TV by now. Plus he'd have to ask me where the fucking keys are. The ones that are hanging right by the door where they always fucking are."

I didn't mean to spill so much, or with so much venom. My face heats as I look away and apologize.

"It's cool, Joannie. I know the type. I've had it, in fact."

She hasn't taken her hand away from mine, yet, but when I look up she's tilted her head slightly, and there's a change in her expression. Like she knows something I don't.

My mouth goes dry for a moment until I remember to close it. I swallow and search for my voice. It was here a minute ago.

"Um, so...that cab?"

"I can do you one better, Joannie." I don't know why, but I love it when she says my name. "Give me your keys and I can drive you home."

"But how will you get to your home?"

She leans forward, a winsome smile curling her pretty mouth. "I *meant* my home."

This can't be happening, surely. I'm used to being hit on at this place. It's just always been dudes.

"I'm, uh...a married woman."

"What you are, Joannie, is fucking sexy. And neglected. And if you're here on a Wednesday night, until closing time, then I dare say you ain't got a lot to go home to."

The ice that forms in my belly is more about how right she is, than how rude. I'm sure my face is the biggest blabbermouth in the world, though. She just smiles even wider, and more hungrily than ever.

"See, Joannie...I know what you need. And it's not just sex, or even orgasms." She reaches over and hooks her fingers into the V-neck of my top, dragging on it until I'm leaning right over toward her.

Her breath caresses my mouth, and I somehow find the words to ask my question. "Oh? And what exactly is it I need?"

She closes the last of the tiny gap between us. When she speaks, her lips glance across mine. "Surrender."

Then she kinks her head and takes my mouth in hers, kissing me so softly it's like I'm dreaming it. Kissing me like no man ever has.

When she glides away, my lips cling to hers for a second, and I forget how to breathe.

"So...what do you say?" she asks.

"C–can you at least tell me your name?"

"Call me Jinx."

Even her name is ten times cooler than I'll ever be. I barely think about what I'm doing as I hand my car keys over to her. They jingle like bells in my trembling grip until she takes hold of them.

Jinx comes out from behind the bar. She takes my hand and puts it around her waist, while she puts her arm over my shoulders. We head out to my car and she even opens the door for me.

It's a short drive to her place, which is probably for the best. If it'd lasted more than 5 minutes I just might have changed my mind.

Jinx comes around and opens my door for me again, and even helps me out. She says nothing, just takes my hand and leads me to her door.

Inside, she puts my keys on a small table, then turns to face me.

"Take off your shoes, Joannie."

I do as I'm told, and the relief for my feet is incredible.

"Come over here, please."

I stumble more than walk, and it's not because of alcohol.

With my stilettos off, I'm now a couple inches shorter than Jinx. When she puts her warm hands on my neck, I gasp at the contact.

Then she leans in and kisses me again. It starts just as softly as at the bar, but it quickly descends into madness.

She parts my lips with hers and thrusts her tongue into my mouth. The prod of her lip stud catches my attention, and I can't help wondering how that hard little thing might feel in…other places.

"Mm," Jinx moans into my mouth. "You're fucking lovely, Joannie."

"Thank you." My voice is so damn tiny.

"Kneel."

"W–what?"

"Get on your knees, sweetmeat." There's a steel in her tone that's not to be argued with. And in a life that's filled with decisions and organization and just fucking coping, being told what to do is the most wonderful release.

I glide down before this gorgeous older woman and gaze up into her eyes. She strokes her inked-up fingers through my hair and I hum with the gentle pleasure of it.

"Wait here, sweetmeat."

She steps past me, and I dare not look. Already I sense I'm supposed to ask permission for...well, anything that I want.

Various rustlings and clunkings sound behind me. Opening of doors, rattling of items, removal of clothes.

When Jinx comes back, she stops right behind me. "Lift your lovely hair."

I obey immediately, bunching my dark locks up on the top of my head.

Suddenly, there's the cool kiss of leather against my neck, and a metallic click at my throat. I've never experienced it, but I know immediately what it is.

A collar.

It's tight enough to make sure I know it's there, but loose enough I can breathe freely.

Jinx comes around in front of me again, and she's an absolute vision. She's stripped down to the most beautiful corset and panties. There's more ink than ever on display and I desperately want to see the rest of it.

She raises her hand and I see she's holding a chain. A chain that's connected to the front of my collar.

"Tell me your name," she says.

"Um...what?"

"Say your name."

At the exact moment I say Joannie, she says it, too. The she follows up with her own name.

"Jinx!"

I furrow my brow and open my mouth to speak, but she presses her finger to my lips. "Uh-uh. I jinxed you. Now you can't speak until I say your name."

Jinx curls the chain around her hand a couple times and then lifts. The collar presses up under my chin and I raise my face in reaction. She bends and presses her mouth to mine, driving her tongue inside me with a long, wet moan.

When she stands straight again, there's a lovely pink in her cheeks that looks almost like a reflection of her lingerie.

"Good girl," she says and turns on the spot. "Come."

I make to stand, but she puts her free hand on my shoulder. "Uh-uh. Hands and knees, sweetmeat."

And so, like a pet, I let her lead me up the hallway to her room. She stops me at the side of her bed and hooks the chain around one post of the bedhead.

Jinx kneels behind me and grips my hips. It's a lot like how my husband does—on the rare occasions he can be bothered to fuck me—only different.

She glides her hands up under my top, her short nails digging into my skin just hard enough to hurt. When she unclasps my bra I think I should maybe protest...but she hasn't said my name, yet.

Jinx slowly undoes the zip in the back of my top and works it and my bra down to the floor. They're both still wrapped around my wrists, and they feel almost like extra restraints.

Then Jinx opens the back of my skirt. She draws it down to my knees, then comes back for my panties.

A moment later, I'm effectively naked, and basically all tied up. Jinx strokes her fingers down my spine, and then dips them between the cheeks of my ass.

The instant she touches my slicked up pussy, I gasp and toss my head back in pleasure.

"No moaning, sweetmeat," she says. "You're under jinx, remember."

She glides one finger up and down my slit, sending sweet tendrils of pleasure through my core. The harder she presses, the wetter I get, and the faster she strokes.

"I'm gonna fuck you so, so well, sweetmeat," she snarls, and I believe her. Why wouldn't I, when she's got me so worked up already with barely anything?

"Stand please," she says, and takes her magical finger away from me.

I catch myself before I whine with need, and then clamber to my feet. Leaving my clothing puddled on the floor.

"My god, you're gorgeous," Jinx says as she gazes over my naked body.

I automatically start to thank her, but she presses her finger to my lips again. The finger she just used to stroke my pussy. My scent is rich on her skin, and though I've never tasted myself before, suddenly it's all I want to do.

Jinx seems to read my mind, and she traces my lips with her wet finger. "Open."

I obey immediately, and she eases it into my mouth. She strokes it over my tongue, and I close around it, drinking my own arousal.

Jinx comes forward and plants her mouth over mine, and we share the taste of me.

Then she steps back and climbs onto her bed. She takes the chain off the bedhead and pulls it. "Come."

She lays me on my back, and straddles my hips. Even with her slender body, she exudes power. Dominance.

Jinx comes forward and I know my eyes widen with surprise. "I want your tongue, sweetmeat."

She still hasn't said my name. I'm not allowed to talk. So, I couldn't say no, even if I wanted to. And I truly don't want to.

Suddenly all I can see is Jinx's pretty plum-colored panties. The sweet and musky scent of her pussy takes hold of my nose, and makes my mouth water.

"Pull them aside, sweetmeat," she moans.

My fingers tremble like crazy as I hook them into the shiny satin. When I pull her panties aside, I pause, gazing in wonder at her rippled lips, with their sheen of wetness.

"Kiss me."

I'm still lost in the moment, so Jinx wraps the chain around her wrist one more loop, and tugs upward. She pulls my mouth in against her pussy, and I have no choice but to open up and stroke her with my tongue.

And as beautiful as it is, to be eating pussy for the first time, the real magic here is in those two words. *No choice.*

She's driving everything about this encounter, and that's making it hotter than anything else I've ever done.

I don't have to decide a single fucking thing. I'm her pet. Her little sweetmeat. And she is in control.

"Yes, that's it," she moans, as I suck on her pretty lips and thrust my tongue inside her. "Oh, god...you're so good, sweetmeat."

I dig my fingers into her thigh, and pull her panties across so hard they rip. Jinx reaches down and pulls them harder until they come completely away, and I dive into her gorgeous cunt for all I'm worth.

"Ohhh...Jesus..." She writhes above me, rolling her hips, painting my face with her sweet juices, and I've never been hornier in my fucking life.

"That's it, sweetmeat...oh, fuck, I'm gonna come..."

I bite into her clit to seal the deal, and she yanks on the chain, and makes a fist in my hair, and cries out as she climaxes.

"Fuck...yes...oh, Joannie...Joannie..."

"Ride my fucking face, mistress," I howl, finally released from the jinx.

My lover moans so beautifully as she comes on my face, and then before I realize what's happening, she throws herself bodily to the side.

When she comes back over me, she's facing the other way. She plants that sweet cunt of hers down on my face again, and drops, landing her beautiful face between my thighs.

The first stroke of her tongue hits me like an electric shock. She pauses for a moment, and then lets out a long, rasping moan.

"Holy fuck, you taste so good, Joannie."

I'm too busy devouring her pussy again, so I just hum out a *thank you*. Jinx hooks her hands around my knees and yanks them back toward my head.

I can feel my pussy gaping and puckering, begging for her mouth. And she doesn't disappoint.

Jinx plows her pretty tongue into me, swirling it inside my cunt as she grinds her chin against my clit. When she prods at my ass with one finger, I pull my mouth away from her and howl with pleasure.

"Oh, sweetmeat," she growls. "You're fucking perfect."

As soon as she finishes speaking, she sucks my clit into her mouth and pumps her finger into my ass. Then, when she drives two fingers into my cunt, I lose my whole fucking mind.

I'm screaming like a banshee as she ignites the sharpest, broadest, punchiest climax I've ever experienced. It slams into me like a runaway building, and I cry out with ragged release, my voice buzzing against her pussy.

I don't know how long it takes before I come back to my senses. All I know is, my legs are curled around Jinx's back, and she's kissing and kissing and fucking kissing my cunt.

After however long it is, this amazing woman rolls off me and lands on her back beside me, her head by my feet.

I reach over and take her hand, and she squeezes back. "Sweetmeat..."

"Jinx...I've never come like that before."

She smiles and wiggles her eyebrows. "But you could again."

I never even planned for this one time to happen. How could it possibly happen again? I have a husband and...and...

"I'd fucking love that, Jinx."

"You know where I work. You know where I live. You come see me anytime you need to...*surrender*, sweetmeat."

THE END

Check out the next book in the series! Heck, why not check out the whole series!?

I have even more F/F erotica on my Steph Brothers pen name. Sign up for my newsletter and keep your finger on my...pulse!

About The Author

Spicy stories of women loving women. Okay, so there's
plenty of red hot lust, too.

Kitty is the sapphic-scribing alter-ego of Steph Brothers.

Made in the USA
Columbia, SC
26 January 2023